Colas Gutman

Merry Christmas, Dumpster Dog!

Illustrated by Marc Boutavant

Translated from French by Claudia Zoe Bedrick

Enchanted Lion Books
BROOKLYN, NY

It is Christmas in Dumpster Dog
and Flat Cat's garbage can. The poor
flattened cat warms himself with
a leaky, hot water bottle, and the
shaggy rug of a dog has put on a
pair of old, holey socks. Dumpster
Dog may be hungry and cold,
but he's still looking forward to
Christmas with happy anticipation.

"I hope we'll be spoiled, Flat Cat!"

"Yes, just like last year, with that

scooter without wheels and the bone without marrow. Frankly, I'm fed up with crummy Christmases, Dumpster Dog."

Dumpster Dog can feel how truly down and deflated his friend Flat Cat is. Hoping to make him feel better, he asks: "What would make you happy, Flat Cat?"

"A brand-new bicycle pump to re-inflate me. How about you, Dumpster Dog?"

"An anti-flea collar and a box of bacon-flavored crackers."

Daydreaming, Dumpster Dog watches crackers dance across his mind. Flat Cat stretches out for a rest in their dumpy home.

"Oh, look, Dumpster Dog, the

well-groomed poodle has a new doo!"

"And the basset has a small winter coat. Why does no one love us, Flat Cat?"

"Because we smell of sardines, Dumpster Dog."

Plummeting, the two friends hit rock bottom. But just then, Dumpster Dog has an idea: "Flat Cat, what if we organize a Christmas for the abandoned?"

"Sure, why not? That way we can

invite all of the neighborhood rats into our garbage can."

"Do you really agree with me?"

"Dumpster Dog, what's with you? You have no ambition. As for me, this year I'm going to spend Christmas Eve at home with an owner. If you wish, follow me!"

Dumpster Dog mopes along through the gutter. He guesses that as long as he smells of sardines, no one will ever invite him in, but Flat Cat reassures him.

"Dumpster Dog, you have your own special dumpy air about you. One Christmas, it's going to pay off."

But finding an owner at home on Christmas Eve who will welcome two poor beasts is like looking for a diamond in a mountain of garbage.

Still, a handwritten sign gives Dumpster Dog a little bit of hope.

NOEL FAMILY
In our home,
it's always Christmas!

Taking his courage in both paws, Dumpster Dog knocks on the door. A girl answers.

"My father isn't here, and my mother has gone out."

But Flat Cat insists, "Have no fear, dear girl. We aren't beasts…"

"Only a Dumpster Dog and a Flat Cat," continues Dumpster Dog.

"Where are your owners?"

"We don't have any," says Flat Cat.

"Come in," says the girl. "In our home, it's always Christmas!"

"Hooray!" says Dumpster Dog.

"Hurrah!" says Flat Cat.

They've hardly made it through the door before the girl exclaims, "Oh, how dirty you are! Well, it's still your lucky day because I don't

have a present for my little brother."

Dumpster Dog can't believe his lucky stars… or fleas. He's going to be a child's Christmas present! Even in his wildest dreams, he'd never imagined such good luck.

He'll throw me a bouncy ball and I'll watch TV while eating mini-sausages. Truly, a good fairy must have magically transformed me into a Labrador! he thinks.

But Flat Cat, who's been burned before, doesn't share Dumpster Dog's enthusiasm.

"She'll give me to her brother as a frisbee, or perhaps a placemat."

"You're sounding like a real show-off, Flat Cat," says Dumpster Dog.

Noel Noel

In her room, the girl prepares to wrap the presents that have suddenly fallen into her lap.

"It won't bother you if I pack you up in garbage bags, will it? I don't want to ruin my wrapping paper."

"Oh, no, we're used to it," says Dumpster Dog, touched and tremendously happy.

"By the way, my name is Marie Noel and my brother is Jean Noel."

"Are you part of Christmas Dog's

family?" says Dumpster Dog.

"Don't mind him," says Flat Cat. "This dog says whatever comes into his head."

"Listen, cat, if my brother ever asks, just say you're a hamster. He adores little rodents."

Marie puts Dumpster Dog and Flat Cat under the tree. Wrapped in his garbage bag, Dumpster Dog can't keep from crying when he thinks of all of the Christmases that he's passed in his smelly garbage can.

"Do you see what's happening, Flat Cat? A child is going to get me as a present!"

"Don't get excited, Dumpster Dog."

"But I'm already excited!"

The children's mother, who

happens to be named Noel Noel,
and their father Pierre Noel invite
the children to open their presents.
  "Marie Noel, Jean Noel, it's time!"

But Jean Noel isn't home yet.

"What is my son doing?" asks Noel Noel.

"I'm sorry," says Jean Noel, who arrives out of breath. "I had to finish my shopping."

Like every Christmas, the parents give their children an up-to-date atlas and encyclopedia. Then they invite them to exchange gifts with each other.

Jean Noel pulls the red tie of a garbage bag and exclaims: "How horrible, a shredded carpet!"

"I'm a dog," says Dumpster Dog.

"And what's that thing, a rat?"

"I'm a hamster," says Flat Cat.

"What do you take me for, a donkey?" says Jean Noel.

Affronted by his presents and
the laughter of his sister, Jean Noel
clenches his teeth and prepares to
take total revenge.

"No point getting upset about it,"
says Pierre Noel. "It's best to accept
the present your sister has given you."

"And anyway," says Dumpster
Dog, "Christmas Dog is the one
who brings the presents."

Now it's Marie Noel's turn to
receive her gifts.

"Holy smokes!" she cries in alarm.

"Did you get a pipe to smoke?"
asks Dumpster Dog.

"No, it's a DWA," says Marie Noel.

"What's that?"

"A doll without arms. And boy is
my brother going to pay dearly for it."

Jean Noel roars with laughter at his
mean joke, while Marie Noel thinks
how she'd like to wring his neck.

"Come on, children, stay calm.
Christmas is a generous holiday,
so let's try to thank each other,"
encourages Pierre Noel.

"Thank you Jean Noel, thank you
Marie Noel, thank you Noel Noel
and Pierre Noel," they say together.

This has given me a dreadful headache,
thinks Dumpster Dog.

With their gifts under their arms,

the siblings head for their rooms. But between brother and sister, war has been declared.

"Where'd you find these horrid animals? On the street?" asks Jean.

"Exactly. How about you: you pull your armless doll from the gutter?"

"Exactly."

"You'll see what I'm going to do to your armless doll! I'm going to rip off its two legs."

"Go ahead—make a DWAx2!"

"A horrible Christmas to you, Jean Noel!"

"A horrible Christmas to you, Marie Noel!"

Dumpster Dog and Flat Cat take refuge in Jean Noel's closet.

"This is still better than our

garbage can," says Flat Cat.

"But I'm afraid, Flat Cat."

"Of what, Dumpster Dog?"

"The armless doll."

(Fair enough, though perhaps it's
the ungrateful children he should
most fear.)

"Hello! Monsters! Where are
you?" calls Jean Noel.

*Oh, good, he wants to play hide and
seek,* thinks Dumpster Dog. *Maybe
he's not so mean after all.*

"Come out immediately or I'll
give you rat poison."

"Darn it," says Dumpster Dog.
"The game's over already."

"Here's the deal," says Jean Noel.
"If you don't want me to sell you this

instant, then you have to obey me. Shredded Carpet: I'm going to train the fleas you have on your coat. And you, rat, you're going to make a nice parachute. I'll tape you to the ceiling and dangle you down from there."

"Dumpster Dog, if we're going to escape, it's now or never."

"Not now, I want to see the show."

"But we *are* the show, dummy!"

Flat Cat pretends to be a rat, because Jean Noel returns with Marie Noel, who is bored stiff by her armless doll.

"She can't vacuum or wash the dishes. She's a big zero. I've thought about it, and I'm willing to trade my DWA for the two monsters," says Marie Noel.

"No way, they're worth far more."

"Big mouth, they're not worth anything at all."

"Well, we'll find out all about that tomorrow," says Jean Noel.

The Christmas Flea Market

Every Christmas Day, the Noel
family sells its old toys and broken
trinkets to raise money for the most
destitute. It's a family tradition. In the
back of Pierre Noel's car, sandwiched
between the robot-arm mixer and
the electric kettle, Dumpster Dog is
enjoying the outing.

"I love garage sales. Once, I found
something that looked just like a
bone with bone marrow in plastic."

The poor dog doesn't yet realize that he belongs to the batch of stuff to be sold.

Mop and second-hand placemat for sale. Offers accepted.

"Kids," says their father. "Enjoy yourselves. I'm going to look for a strainer."

While Dumpster Dog wonders whether he might be lucky enough to find a second-hand anti-flea collar, his old acquaintances appear before him.

"What are you doing here?" asks the well-groomed poodle.

"Selling," says Dumpster Dog.

"Really? What are you selling?"
asks the basset in his little winter coat.

"A doll without arms," replies
Dumpster Dog.

"She's just horrible!" exclaims

the basset. "Would you let me take a picture for my mother? She's crazy about horrible things."

"It's a garage sale, not a garbage dump," sneers the well-groomed poodle.

Dumpster Dog and Flat Cat watch the happy children passing by, but no one pays any attention to their stand. No one, that is, except a girl in a large pullover sweater.

"Oh, look at that poor thing! She doesn't even have a coat!" says the basset, snug in his own small coat.

"Nor a proper set of bangs," says the well-groomed poodle.

The girl approaches, trembling with cold, and says: "That doll is mine, it's my armless doll!"

"Oh, sure. And I'm Father Christmas," says Jean Noel.

"Father Christmas? Who's that?" asks Dumpster Dog.

"I found it a year ago in a garbage can," continues the girl.

"If you want this doll without arms, it's going to cost you an arm and a leg!" laughs Marie Noel.

"But I don't have any money."

"Do you have something to trade?" asks Jean Noel.

"Two potatoes."

"Thanks, but we have some already."

"That's odd, I don't' see any here," says Dumpster Dog.

Poor pullover-sweater girl, thinks Dumpster Dog. He wants to lick her feet to comfort her, but he's forgotten that he's attached like a bicycle to a post.

Fortunately, Christmas is just a little bit different from other days.

"If you want the armless doll, you can always make a run for it," suggests Marie Noel. "Or take that smelly, shredded carpet, if you want. After all, it's Christmas."

"But I have no use for it."

"You can always swap it for a doormat," says Jean Noel.

"Can my cat come with me?" asks Dumpster Dog, who finally understands that they're talking about him.

"For now," says Jean Noel.

Behind a crate of broken bottles, Dumpster Dog makes the proper introductions.

"I'm Dumpster Dog and this is my friend Flat Cat."

"I thought you were a mop and a hot plate!"

"It's okay, it happens all the time," says Dumpster Dog.

"But I won't be able to feed you. I'm very poor," says the girl.

"Please don't worry. We're familiar with garbage cans and their riches."

Thank you, Christmas Dog, thinks Dumpster Dog. *Thank you for giving me this child. She may not be rich, but she has a good heart.*

Cat's Pajamas!

In a small shack, over a bowl of soup
with a single vegetable, a crust of
bread, and a cheese crumb, Pullover
recounts her sad story.

"I was begging in front of the
church with my armless doll and
fell asleep. When I woke up, she was
nowhere to be found."

"That is very sad," says Dumpster
Dog, a tear in his eye.

"But why do you beg, Pullover?"
asks Flat Cat.

"My father is blind and my mother is deaf, and they are unable to work."

"What happened to them?" asks Flat Cat.

"They worked their whole lives for mean people who forced them to use bad cleaning products. My father went blind because of it, and my mother went deaf on account of being yelled at. Look, here they are, back from the dump."

"Hello," says Dumpster Dog.

"Is that your armless doll sleeping?" asks her blind father.

"What are you saying?" asks the deaf mother.

"I've brought home two friends," says Pullover.

"Let me touch them," says her
father. "A nice mop and a mat."

"I'll mop the floor and your
mother will set out the soup. You
can play with your armless doll
while you wait."

Because Pullover no longer has her doll, she begins to cry.

It's so unfair! thinks Dumpster Dog. *We have to get her DWA back!*

Even if Dumpster Dog hadn't had the good fortune to play much fetch in his life, he had gotten good training as a dog detective, tracking down sandwich crusts. Wanting answers, he opens an investigation and questions Pullover.

"Where did you last see your doll?"

"At the market."

"Oh, okay, that's odd, since we were just there. At which stand?"

"Yours."

"What a coincidence!" says Dumpster Dog, who has no memory.

"Apart from her missing arms,

does your doll have anything else to
distinguish her from other armless
dolls?"

"No."

"That's a pity."

"Wait… she does. I engraved a
heart on her left thigh."

"I have what I need, Flat Cat!

Let's get to work."

"You are the cat's pajama's, Dumpster Dog, if you already know where to look for that doll."

"I don't, Flat Cat, but I like hearts an awful lot."

"As far as I see it," says Flat Cat, "she's back home with the infamous Noel family."

"If nobody bought her at the flea market," says Pullover, worried.

"Please don't worry," says Flat Cat.

Together, Dumpster Dog and Flat Cat pledge to find Pullover's armless doll. Then, they fall asleep, like a cat and a dog, curled up against her scratchy sweater.

Leftovers Day

Upon awakening, Dumpster Dog
prances about with impatience.

"Ready to go, Flat Cat?"

"Calm down, doggie. Let's eat."

"Pullover, you stay and eat your
breadless, butterless, jamless breakfast.
We're going to go dumpster diving,
but will be back soon. Flat Cat is
right: A good dog detective amounts
to nothing with an empty stomach."

"People really throw away just about anything, Dumpster Dog. Look, a four-pound knish!"

Such happiness! Such joy! thinks Dumpster Dog.

"What's this orange thingy?" says Flat Cat.

"An orange?" asks Dumpster Dog.

"No, silly, it's a pumpkin. And who, might I ask, usually likes pumpkins?"

"Dunno. Cat got my tongue."

"I really wish I didn't have to tell you, but I will anyway: children!"

"Children like pumpkins?"

"Of course, for Halloween."

"You want to give Pullover a pumpkin to wear?"

"Of course not, but it's perfect for that horrible child Jean Noel. Just think!"

"Why?" asks Dumpster Dog.

"We'll trade it for his DWA!"

After going back to get Pullover, they head for the Noels' house.

In our home, it's always Christmas.

Garbage Can Treasures

Dumpster Dog is dressed up as a pumpkin and Flat Cat sports a fine set of vampire teeth. They're a perfect Halloween duo.

Pullover hides behind a pine tree, ready to surprise the enemy.

"Ding-dong," says Dumpster Dog.

"Nothing will happen if you just imitate the sound of a bell, Dumpster Dog. You've got to knock on the door."

"My father isn't here, and my mother has gone out," says Marie Noel.

"We've found a Halloween costume," says Dumpster Dog. "A garbage can treasure."

"Jean Noel, it's for you!"

Unfortunately, Flat Cat's clever plan falls completely flat.

"Dad, Mom—help! The trash has returned!" calls Jean Noel.

"The word is 'trespasser'" replies their father. "Children, stay calm."

"They want to trade my doll without arms for a pumpkin outfit they found in the garbage, which isn't fair because my doll is worth more. And it's not even the right season for a pumpkin."

"It's MY doll without arms," corrects Marie Noel.

"No, it's mine!" declares Pullover, popping out suddenly from behind the tree.

"Can someone explain to me what is going on?" asks their mother.

Christmas with a Heart

Flat Cat and Dumpster Dog take
their places in the large library that
doubles as a living room. Flat Cat is
so overcome with emotion that he
has a frog in his throat and is unable
to say a word. As for Dumpster Dog,
he's too afraid of the doll without
arms to say anything. So, it's left to
Pullover to defend herself.

"I was begging near the church
and fell asleep," says Pullover.

"Yeah, well, I play on my bed and get sleepy, but I don't go spilling my life story to people!" says Jean Noel.

"When I woke up, my doll was gone," continues Pullover.

"What a party pooper," says Jean Noel. "Mom, Dad, don't listen to this silly, stinky girl."

"My dear, your story is truly heartbreaking," says Noel Noel, "but there's nothing to prove that the doll is yours."

Pullover trembles, unsure of what to say next. Dumpster Dog's eyes are still lowered so he doesn't have to see the armless doll. But he knows that he has to intervene as quickly as he possibly can.

"Tell us, Pullover, what did you engrave on your doll?" says Dumpster Dog.

"A little heart on her left thigh."

Pierre Noel takes the doll by the leg and is dumbfounded to discover the engraved heart.

"My word, she's right! It *is* her doll without arms!"

"This is just terrible! Jean Noel, how could you steal a doll from a homeless girl?" asks Noel Noel.

"Well, she was asleep and her doll was dangling down into the gutter. I thought it would be a nice gift for Marie Noel. Anyway, it's worth more than these nasty animals!"

"Children, we are going to have to crack down and punish you," says their mother.

"Oh, don't be too severe," says Dumpster Dog. "It's Christmas!"

Like a great prince bestowing favors, Dumpster Dog places his pumpkin costume from the dumpster at Jean Noel's feet.

"Next time, look in the dumpsters rather than the gutters, you big boob!" says Flat Cat.

"In any case, I've had it with this doll without arms," says Marie Noel. "I'll wait for the DWAx5: without arms, legs, hair, ears, and neck!"

A Garbage Can Tale

Christmas isn't quite over for
Dumpster Dog and Flat Cat. They
still have to say goodbye to Pullover,
before returning to their smelly
garbage can.

"Goodbye, Pullover, and don't
catch cold," says Dumpster Dog.

"Thank you, dear friends. Thanks
to you, I've had a beautiful Christmas."

Now, all that's needed for
Christmas to be truly perfect is for

something miraculous to occur, like a chance meeting on a street corner.

"We've been looking all over for you," says the well-groomed poodle.

"I showed the photo of your doll to my mother," says the basset. "She saw the same one in *Hot Dog* magazine."

"It's a collectible doll," explains the well-groomed poodle.

"A collectible?" asks Pullover.

"Yes, it's rare and valuable. You will be very rich!"

"As long as I'm alive, I will never sell my doll!" says Pullover.

"Come on, at least a leg. I'm sure you have need of money."

Pullover thinks about how her parents could go to the doctor and regain their sight and hearing.

Then, good-naturedly, she removes her doll's left leg, the one with the little heart engraved on the thigh. She will sell it to the mother of the basset in the little coat.

After, Dumpster Dog and Flat Cat make their way home, as delighted with their adventures as with the two garbage bags they see waiting

for them in their garbage can, the red
ties pulled into bows.

"Do you think he's come, Flat Cat?"
"Who?"
"Christmas Dog"
"Dream on, Cinderella."
"It's me, Flat Cat. Dumpster Dog."
Though it's out of character, the
old, stinky dog happens to be right:
Christmas Dog *has* visited their

garbage can, leaving Flat Cat a new
bicycle pump to reinflate himself,
and Dumpster Dog the anti-flea
collar of which he's dreamed.

All that remains is for them to
uncork an empty bottle to celebrate
Christmas in style.

"Merry Christmas, Flat Cat!"

"Merry dumpster, Dumpster Dog!"

www.enchantedlion.com

First English-language edition published in 2019
by Enchanted Lion Books,
67 West Street, Ste 403, Brooklyn, NY 11222
Originally published in French as *Joyeux Noël, Chien Pourri!*
Copyright © 2013 by l'école des loisirs, Paris, France
Copyright © 2019 by Enchanted Lion Books
for the English-language translation & edition
Production and layout: Elynn Cohen and Sarah Klinger
All rights reserved under International and
Pan-American Copyright Conventions
A CIP record is on file with the Library of Congress
ISBN 978-1-59270-271-8 (hardcover)
ISBN 978-1-59270-273-2 (paperback)

1 3 5 7 9 8 6 4 2

Printed in the US by Worzalla, Stevens Point, WI

First Printing